Dalmatian Press

The DALMATIAN PRESS name, logo, and Tear and Share are trademarks of Dalmatian Press, Franklin, Tennessee 37067. DalmatianPress.com. No part of this book may be reproduced or copied in any form without the written permission of Dalmatian Press and Disney Enterprises, Inc. All rights reserved.

21445 Doc McStuffins Gigantic Book to Color
13 14 15 CLI 39178 10 9 8 7 6 5 4 3 2 1

D1450010

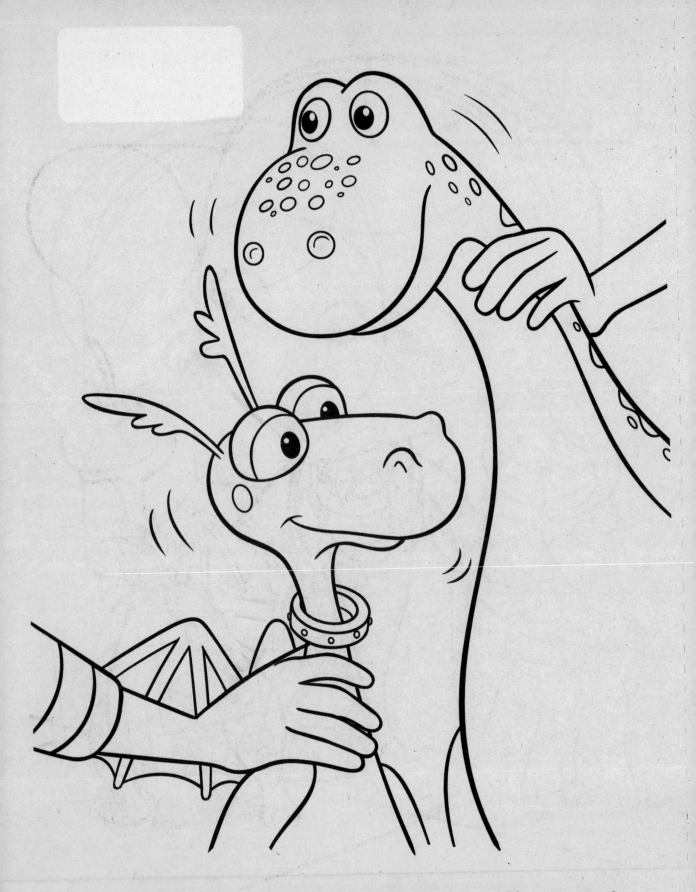

Doc and Donny are playing with their stuffed animals.
"Roar!" says Bronty.

2

"Ah!" says Doc. "Run away, Stuffy!"

Dalmatian Press

"Doc! Donny!" calls Dad. "Time for lunch."

"My salami sandwich is great, Dad," says Donny.

Dalmatian Press

"Here, Bronty," says Donny. "Have some salami!"

6

"Finish up, Donny," says Mom.
"I'll take you to soccer practice."

Circle the items that begin with the letter B.

Answers: bananas, bread, basket, butter, blender, bottle, bowls, ball, book, box, bag

8

"We'll be in the backyard, Dad!" says Doc.

"This is fun," says Lambie. "Let's go, Bronty!"

"Hey, Lenny," says Bronty.

"Sorry," says Lenny. "I have to go!"

"I wonder why Lenny ran away," says Lambie.

Dalmatian Press

"I don't know!" says Bronty, breathing on Lambie.

"Bronty, your breath is smelly!" says Lambie.

"Time for a checkup!" says Doc.

"But I feel fine," says Bronty.

"You have bad breath, Bronty," says Hallie.

"I'm going to give you a dental checkup," says Doc.

"Open wide!"

"You have a piece of salami stuck in
your teeth," says Doc.

"You have stinkysalamibreath!" says Doc.

22

"Let's add that to the Big Book of Boo Boos!"

"We can treat this with a toothbrush and toothpaste!"

"That didn't hurt a bit!" says Bronty.

"Your breath is minty-fresh, Bronty!" says Lenny.
"Let's play!"

"Thanks, Doc!"

Doc and her friend Henry are ready
to watch a meteor shower.

"Anyone want a star cookie?" asks Dad.

Henry has a new telescope.

"What do you see?" asks Doc. "A star?
Two stars? A whole galaxy?"

"I can't see a thing!" says Henry. "Everything is fuzzy."

"I'll see if I can fix it," says Doc.

"Better hurry," says Dad.
"The meteor shower will start soon!"

"Hi, Hallie," says Doc.
"Meet Aurora, our new patient!"

"This place is great," says Aurora.

"Oh, sorry!" says Aurora. "Didn't see you there."

"Nice doggie!" says Aurora.

"You need an eye exam," says Doc.

"Tell me what you see on this eye chart," says Doc.

"Pretzels!" says Aurora.

"I have a diagnosis!" shouts Doc.
"Aurora has Blurrystaritis!"

"Can you help her see better?" asks Lambie.

"Doctors give kids—and hippos—
glasses to help them see," says Doc.

44

"I'll say!"

"I think I see the problem!" says Doc.
"Your eyepiece is missing!"

"I wonder what happened to it," says Lambie.

"Here it is!" says Stuffy. "I found it!"

"This eyepiece will help you see clearly," says Doc.

"Everything is so clear!" says Aurora. "And close!"

"I fixed the telescope!" says Doc.
"Just in time!" says Dad.

"The meteor shower is happening!" shouts Henry.
"Thanks, Doc!"

Dalmatian Press

Welcome to the family, Sofia!

Princess Amber and Prince James are twins.

All hail Princess Sofia!

Which picture of Sofia is different?

A

B

C

D

All hail Princess Sofia!

Answer: B

King Roland says there will be a ball in Sofia's honor.

The king gives Sofia the Amulet of Avalor.
She promises to always wear it!

Cedric, The Royal Sorcerer

Cedric wants Sofia's magic amulet.

"The amulet is so pretty, Sofia. May I hold it?"
asks Cedric.

The Magic Amulet
Find the best words to complete the rhyme.

For each deed performed, for better or
_____ .

Which word comes next?

Word   Work   Worse

A power is granted, a blessing or

_____ .

Which word comes next?

Care   Curse   Call

Answers: Worse, Curse

"Oh, Merlin's mushrooms!" says Cedric.

Will Sofia be ready for the ball?
She doesn't know how to dance.

James tries to teach Sofia to dance.

Complete the number pattern in the dance steps.

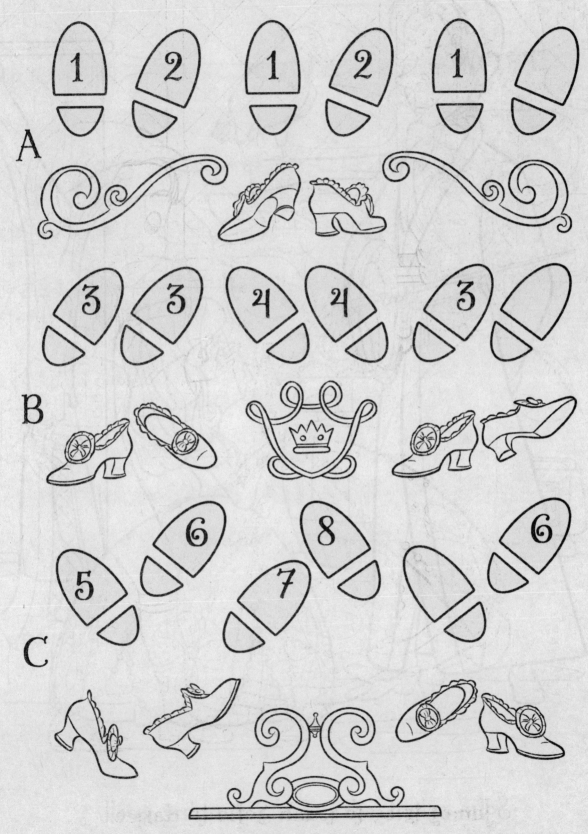

A

B

C

Answers: A-2, B-3, C-5

© Disney

Sofia asks Cedric for a dancing spell

Cedric wants to trick Sofia and take the amulet.

Sofia hopes the spell works!

Draw what Cedric is thinking about.

When Cedric's spell backfires, Sofia gets
a quick dance lesson from Amber!

Princess Sofia

Delmarian Press

Sofia dances with the king.

Decode the message by matching the letters to the numbers.

Sof___ ___ d___nc___d
3   1   1   2

l___k___ ___ r___ ___l
3   2   1   2   1

pr___nc___ss!
3   2

1=a   2=e   3=i

Princess Sofia wakes up.

Time to get dressed.

Help Sofia find her way to the dining hall

Start

Baileywick takes Sofia to breakfast.

So many choices!

Time for school.

The Royal Coach

Connect the dots to complete the flying horse.

© Disney

Welcome to Royal Prep—the Royal Preparatory Academy

Headmistresses Flora, Fauna, and Merryweather

Amber's best friends—Clio and Hildegard

Unscramble the names!

O F A S I

_ _ _ _ _

EMRBA

_ _ _ _ _

OLIC

_ _ _ _

MESAJ

_ _ _ _ _

Dalmatian Press

© Disney

Hurry to class.

Every princess must know how to curtsy.

Arts & Crafts

Draw what Sofia is painting.

Dalmatian Press

Sofia makes new friends at Royal Prep.

Professor Popov's Dance Class

Recess!

Good Morning!
Put the pictures in order by numbering them 1-4.

A

B

_____

C

_____

D

_____

_____

Dalmatian Press

Answers: 1-B, 2-A, 3-D, 4-C

Amber and Clio share a secret.

Dalmatian Press

A

Hildegard gets an "A" in Fan Fluttering.

Dalmatian Press

Time to Study

Find and circle 4 pictures of Sofia and 3 books.

Dalmatian Press

Be careful, Sofia!

Magic Class

Learning to be a princess is not easy!

Home Sweet Home

Dalmatian Press

Find and circle 7 items that begin with the letter B.

A Royal Tea Party

Oops!

Amber wonders if Sofia will ever be a real princess.

Match the shadows to their owners.

1

2

3

A

B

C

Answers: 1-C, 2-A, 3-B

108

Baileywick announces that dinner is served.

Sofia has so much to learn!

Count the tableware.

How many forks do you see?

How many knives do you see?

How many spoons do you see?

Add all the silverware together.

Answers: 6 forks, 3 knives, 3 spoons; Total = 12

"How was your day, dear?"

Sofia misses her village friends.

Ruby and Jade

A Royal Sleepover

There are 6 differences between the two pictures. Can you find them?

Answers: 1- Clover, 2- cake instead of tea in Sofia's hand, 3- teapot, 4- table legs, 5- saucer missing, 6- curler missing

116

A Magical Puppet Show

Dalmatian Press

A Royal Makeover

Best Friends Forever!

Homework with Vivian—Build a Dream Castle

Draw your own Dream Castle.

Look down and across to find the words listed below.

```
M O M S O F I A R
I J B R O B I N O
R A M B E R N C L
A M G B K U G C A
N E O U F B P L N
D S E P J Y Q O D
A T Y N A D Z V E
H W A I D J U E Y
H I L D E G A R D
```

Amber
Clover
Hildegard
Miranda
Robin

Roland
Jade
Ruby
James
Sofia

Crackle!

New Friends

Crackle's Special Talent

Find and circle 5 pictures of Crackle and 3 pictures of corn.

The Tri-Kingdom Picnic

Princess Jun and Prince Jin from Wei-Ling

Prince Khalid and Princess Maya from Khaldoun.

The Prince and Princesses of Enchancia!

Unscramble the words.

CINPER

_ _ _ _ _ _

LCSTAE

_ _ _ _ _ _

INCCIP

_ _ _ _ _ _

OGKIDNM

_ _ _ _ _ _ _

SSPCNEIR

_ _ _ _ _ _ _ _

Dalmatian Press

Answers: prince, castle, picnic, kingdom, princess

The Flying Horseshoe Toss

The princesses work on their parasol.

Golden Egg on a Silver Spoon Race

The best team wins the Golden Chalice. Connect the dots to complete the trophy.

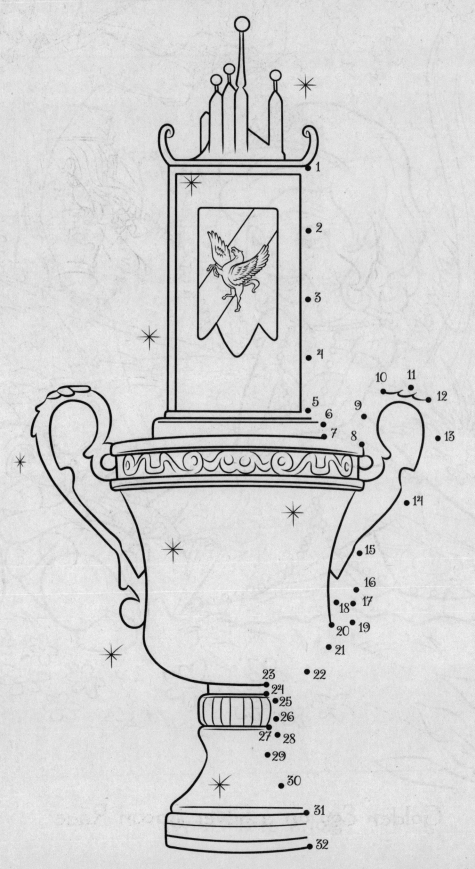

Sofia and Clover

Robin and Mia

Whatnaught

Hide and Seek
Find and circle the 10 animals.

Dalmatian Press

The Flying Derby is about to begin.

Sofia and Minimus

Prince Hugo bumps into Sofia!

Help Sofia and Minimus win the race!

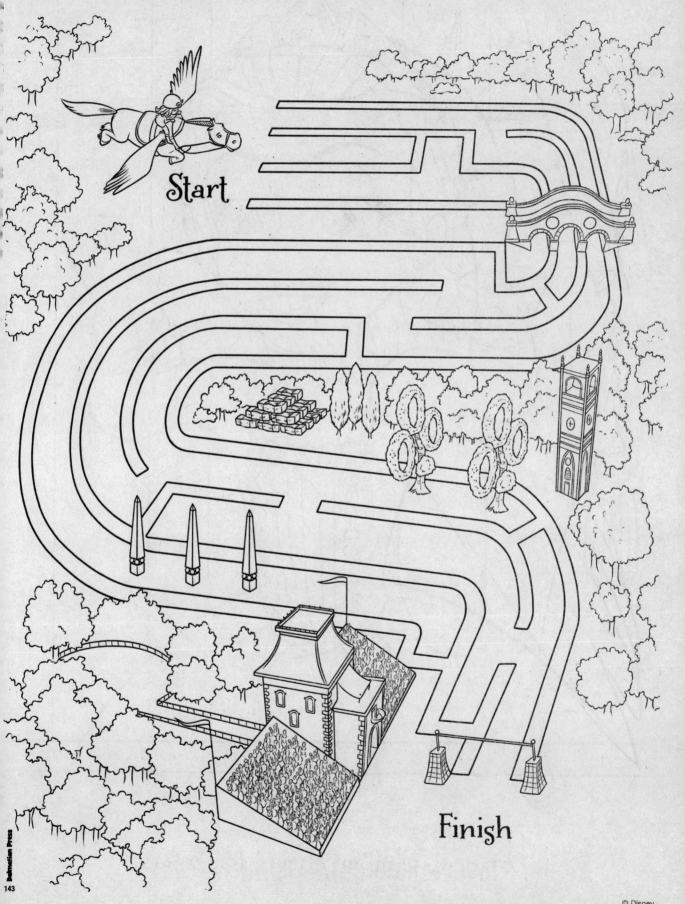

Start

Finish

Princess Amber cheers for Sofia.

Sofia wins!

Count the flying horses!

The Royal Family Portrait

Hooray for Princess Sofia the First!

MICKEY MOUSE CLUBHOUSE

"What shall I wear?"

Daisy is looking lovely.

"Look at my new ring!"

How sparkly!

Minnie loves a bit of bling.
Draw some of your favorite pieces of jewelry.

154

Don't be BAAAShful

Butterflies look like bows.

Super cute!

Oops!

Dalmatian Press

funny bunny

What a cutie!

162

Let's have a
tea party

A purse adds a pop of color.

Minnie and Daisy love to shop!
Draw your favorite dress or outfit.

Help Minnie design the perfect outfit.

Color the dress, purse, and shoes.

Dalmatian Press

Bath Time

The bubbles are everywhere!

Twirly Girl

Let's take a road trip!

It's playtime!

Tweet-tweet-tweet!

Which piece completes the picture?

A
B
C

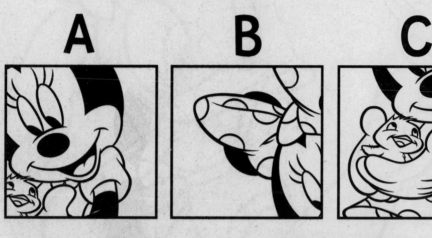

Your Answer:

Answer: A

All dolled up!

Picture Perfect

How sweet!

Dalmatian Press

How lovely!

What's your favorite color?

Minnie loves her pets!
Draw a picture of your favorite animal.

Make a list of things you love.

I Love . . .

_____

_____

_____

_____

_____

_____

_____

"What a beautiful day!"

kites
are flowers in the
sky

Dalmatian Press

"A pretty bow for you!"

A bicycle built for two!

© Disney

Decorate the cupcake!

Bows are Minnie's favorite accessory!
Color the bows.

Fresh fruit from the garden!

Breezy Day

190

Find and circle 4 differences in the two pictures.

Answers: Minnie's tail is missing, the leash is missing, spots on the dog are missing, Minnie's button is missing.

A wonderful day for friends to play.

Daisy likes cupcakes.

BLING!

Look up, down, across, and diagonally for these fun, sparkly blings.

BEADS
BELT
BOWS

BRACELET
GEM
JEWEL

NECKLACE
PURSE
RING

R	✳	B	O	W	S	B	N
I	T	O	J	E	W	E	L
N	💍	N	A	S	C	A	B
G	E	M	✳	K	I	D	E
W	F	D	L	P	💍	S	L
B	R	A	C	E	L	E	T
H	C	💍	V	J	B	✳	A
E	R	B	P	U	R	S	E

Draw what Daisy is thinking about.

"A pretty bow for me!"

Use the grid to draw Minnie Mouse.

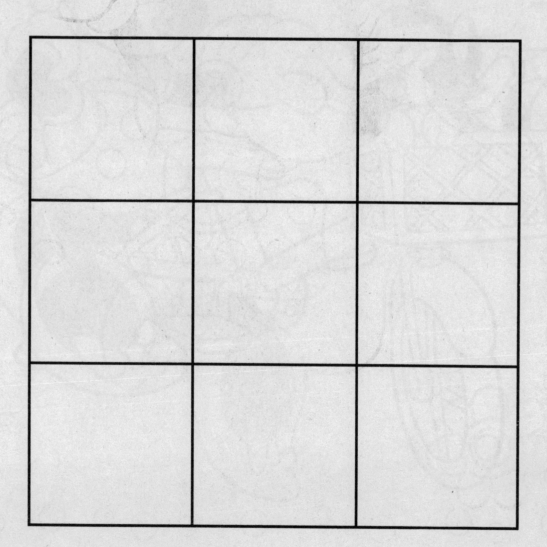

Dalmatian Press

Where shall we go?

I'm ready to roll!

Draw a new kite for Minnie.

200

Dalmatian Press

Mickey and Minnie pal around all day. Draw pictures of their silly afternoon.

at the park . . .

eating a snack . . .

SHOPPING SPREE!

You've won a shopping spree at your favorite store. Draw some cool things you would buy.

Friends Forever

Ellyvan has come to play soccer.
No one else is there.

Taxicrab is making smoothies for his friends.
They have just finished a game of soccer.
Where was Ellyvan?

Oh, dear! The game was played in the morning.
Ellyvan came in the afternoon!

Bungo tells Ellyvan about the goal he scored to win the game.

Tomorrow is the day for the big Coconut Run Road Race. "Don't be late, Ellyvan!" says Taxicrab.

Zoom! The Coconut Run Road Race is under way.

Toadhog and Zooter near the finish line!

Zooter wins! Connect the dots to complete the picture.

Hooray for Zooter!

Miss Jolly and the Beetlebugs are going to check on Ellyvan. He missed the race!

"I went to the starting line this morning but no one else was there," says Ellyvan. "So I came home."

"You were too early!" says Miss Jolly. "The race was in the afternoon, not the morning."

Bungo made signs to help Ellyvan learn the parts of the day. Number the signs in this order: Morning, Afternoon, and Night.

Morning is when Ellyvan eats his breakfast of cereal and fruit.

Dalmatian Press

"Afternoon starts with lunchtime and goes all the way to suppertime," says Bungo.

"The picnic is tomorrow afternoon, Ellyvan,"
says Hippobus. "Don't forget!"

The next day, Ellyvan is right on time for the picnic.
Where is everyone else?

"You're right on time!" everyone shouts.

What a wonderful picnic!
"Hooray!" says Ellyvan. "I was hungry!"